Original Cat, Copy Cat

SARAH KURPIEL

GREENWILLOW BOOKS
An Imprint of HarperCollinsPublishers

For Mom.

And for Comet and Cad too.

Original Cat, Copy Cat
Copyright © 2021 by Sarah Kurpiel
All rights reserved. Manufactured in Italy.
For information address HarperCollins Children's Books,
a division of HarperCollins Publishers, 195 Broadway, New York, NY 10007.
www.harpercollinschildrens.com

The illustrations were created digitally. The text type is EffectraThin.

Library of Congress Cataloging-in-Publication Data

Names: Kurpiel, Sarah, author, illustrator.
Title: Original cat, copy cat / written and illustrated by Sarah Kurpiel.
Description: First edition. | New York, NY : Greenwillow Books, an Imprint of HarperCollins Publishers, [2021] |
Audience: Ages 4–8. | Audience: Grades K–1. | -Summary: "Pineapple's entire routine is turned upside down
when new kitten Kiwi copies everything Pineapple does. But eventually Pineapple learns
that having a friend makes everything better"— Provided by publisher.
Identifiers: LCCN 2020025918 | ISBN 9780062943835 (hardcover)
Subjects: CYAC: Cats—Fiction. | Animals—infancy—Fiction. | Friendship—Fiction.
Classification: LCC PZ7.1.K87 Ori 2021 | DDC [E]—dc23 LC record available at https://lccn.loc.gov/2020025918
First Edition

21 22 23 24 25 RTLO 10 9 8 7 6 5 4 3 2 1

Greenwillow Books

Pineapple had always been the only cat.

He had a comfortable life
and a sweet routine—

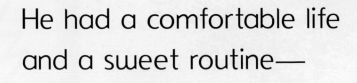

until he wasn't
the only cat anymore.

Kiwi was fast.

Kiwi was LOUD.

Kiwi
was
exhausting.

Everywhere
Pineapple went,
Kiwi went too.

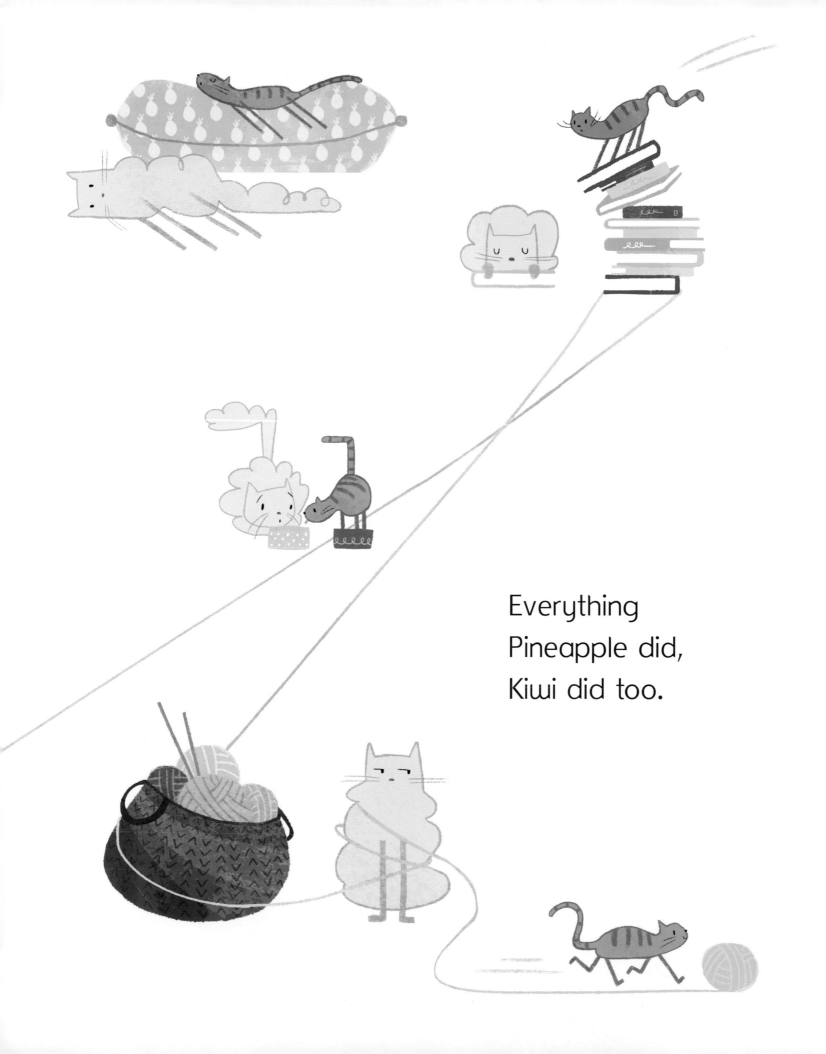

Everything
Pineapple did,
Kiwi did too.

Every spot Pineapple loved,
Kiwi loved too.

One day . . .

enough
was
enough.

Kiwi zoomed
out of sight.

Finally, Pineapple
could get back
to his comfortable life.

But his sweet routine
had soured.
The house grew
quieter
and quieter.

Too quiet.

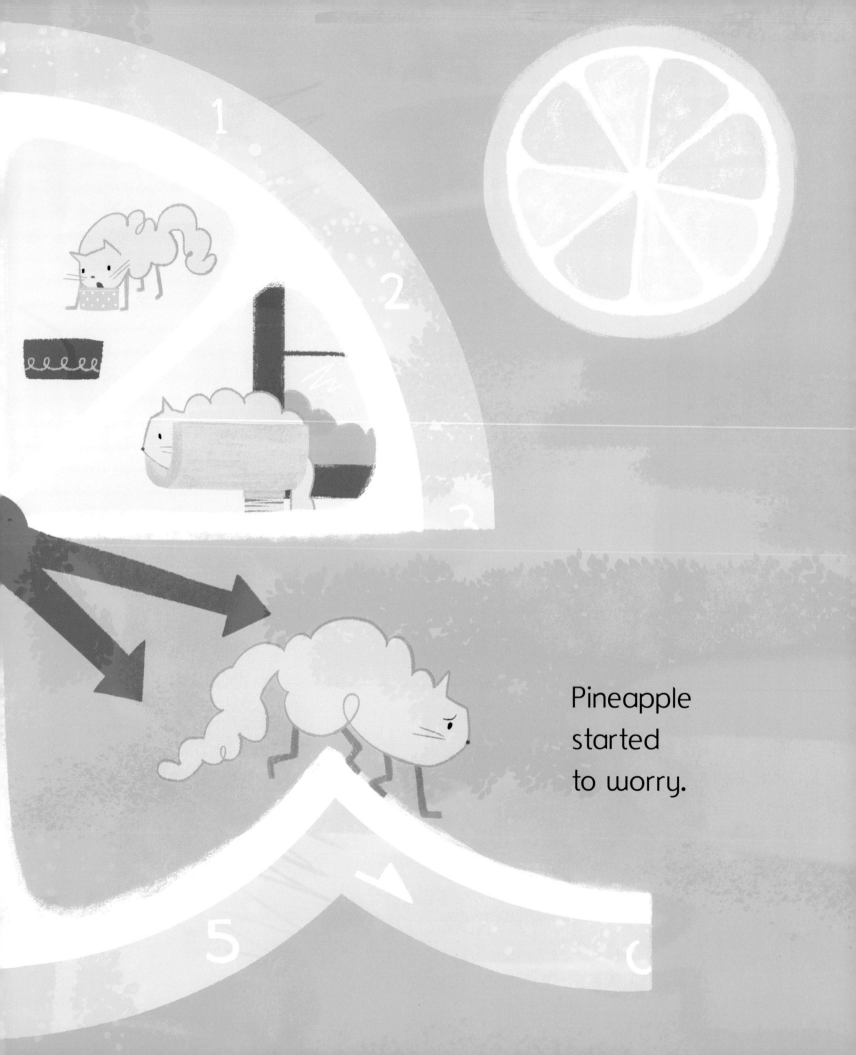

Pineapple
started
to worry.

He searched under

and over,

in bright,
shiny places

and dark, dusty places,

until he saw a small,
striped tail.

Was
Kiwi
stuck?

Pineapple went in to check.

Kiwi was not stuck.

Next Kiwi leaped
onto the railing.
What if he slipped?

Pineapple hopped up to keep
an eye on him. Kiwi did not slip.

And when Kiwi disappeared,
Pineapple worried he might get lost.

So he crept in too.

Kiwi was not lost.

Pineapple had never seen
the world like this before.

From then on,
everything Kiwi did,
Pineapple did too.

Or was it
the other way
around?

Maybe they were both copycats.
Your guess is as good as mine.